Myths, Legends and Monsters

By Mick Gowar

Illustrated by Andrew Bylo

LONGMAN

CONTENTS

THE SPHINX

THE SPHINX

Night was falling fast on the high, mountain road that led to the great city of Thebes. A weary traveller was hurrying to reach the safety of the city before darkness fell. Everyone, for many miles around, had heard tales of spice merchants, camel drivers – even soldiers – vanishing before they could reach the city. Mount Phicium was no place to be when darkness fell.

The traveller quickened his pace. Only two more miles to go. Suddenly, he heard a rushing sound, like the beating of enormous wings. Terrified by the thought of what monster might make such a dreadful noise, he broke into a run, only to trip and stumble over something that felt like a large, round rock.

The traveller picked himself up and looked back. It wasn't a rock that had tripped him, it was a skull: a human skull. He looked about him. All around were bones, bleached white by the sun – human bones!

"Good evening, friend," said a pleasant voice.

Stifling a scream, the traveller looked up. Gazing down at him was an enormous creature. From the waist up she had the body of a giantess, but from the waist down she had the hindquarters of an enormous lion.

"Wh – Wh – What are you?"

"I am the Sphinx," replied the enormous creature. "And rather than waste either of our time, I will tell you straight away that I eat human flesh.

"Don't scream like that – it won't do you the slightest good. We are at least two miles from Thebes, and with my reputation –" the Sphinx added, in her matter of fact way, "even if someone *did* hear you, the very last thing they would do is come and help you.

"And *don't* try to run away. I could leap on you and tear you apart before you got two metres, and I really don't want to do that. I am so strong and powerful, and you are so puny; it wouldn't be sporting, would it?"

The poor man was too astonished and terrified to say anything.

"I suggest a little wager," continued the Sphinx, in her reasonable tone. "I will ask you a riddle. If you answer it correctly you can go on your way unharmed. If, however, you don't get it right, I eat you for supper. Agreed?"

"Er. Y – y – y – yes," replied the terrified traveller. He could see he had no choice.

"Splendid!" said the Sphinx, and she winked one golden eye and licked her thin, cruel lips. "Here is the riddle: what creature has its tail between its eyes?"

"I – I – I – I ... bi – bi – bi ... " the poor man was almost speechless with fear.

"Come on, man! Pull yourself together!" scolded the Sphinx. "I'll say it again: what creature has its tail between its eyes?"

The Sphinx lazily lifted a front foot to her mouth and began to lick the claws that gleamed like butchers' knives at the end of her enormous paw.

"I – I – I – I ... " babbled the traveller.

"Useless!" complained the Sphinx. "Absolutely useless! Watch –"

She lifted her tail and began to lick a small scratch high up on her right hind leg. As she did so, her tail flopped down over her head and dangled in front of her face and between her eyes. After a minute or two of licking, she flicked her tail to one side.

"Peek-a-boo," said the Sphinx playfully. "I spy with my little eye something to eat for my dinner!"

The tentmaker sighed with relief. He could see the walls of Thebes in the distance, no more than two miles away. He dug his heels sharply into the donkey's flanks and urged it into a loping trot.

"Good day, friend," said a melodious voice from above.

The tentmaker looked up into the face of the Sphinx.

"I am the Sphinx," said the Sphinx. "Guess what I eat?"

"Er, m – m – mountain g – goats?" asked the petrified tentmaker.

"No!" said the Sphinx with a sneer. "There are no mountain goats round here. "Think, man: what comes along here that is meaty, succulent and very, very stupid?"

"D – donkeys?" suggested the tentmaker hopefully.

"Getting warmer," said the Sphinx, encouragingly. "You've got one guess left. I'll give you one last clue: what rides donkeys and begins with a 'T'?"

"T – t – t – tentmakers?" the poor man stammered.

"Mmmmm," said the Sphinx thoughtfully. "I was actually thinking of 'travellers', but I'll accept 'tentmakers'. Congratulations! Now for the question that could save your life – are you ready, tentmaker?"

"Please don't hurt me!" screamed the tentmaker. "Let me live – *please* let me live!"

"Here is the riddle – " announced the Sphinx, ignoring the pleas of the terrified tentmaker.

But the poor tentmaker was far too frightened to play games. "Let me go, please let me go!" he shrieked. "Take my donkey, take my money – you can even take my tents! But please – please – I beg of you, don't hurt me … ."

"Oh dear," sighed the Sphinx as she washed her paws a little while later. "*What a piece of wimp is man.* He was even less fun than the other fellow – but much tastier!"

Laius, King of Thebes, swerved his chariot out of the palace and viciously whipped the frightened horses into top speed. The chariot hurtled down the broad road towards the great gates of the city. The two guards who were with him clung on to the sides of the chariot. His majesty was in a foul mood as usual.

For three long weeks no one had been able to leave or enter the city for fear of the dreadful thing that waited in the mountains. Rumours had been spreading of a monstrous beast – half-woman, half-lion – which had been seen basking on the summit of Mount Phicium. Laius knew that such a creature could only have been sent by one of the gods as a punishment – but which god, and to punish what crime? Laius had no idea. There was only thing to do, Laius knew: consult the great oracle at Delphi. Only the python priestess, who knew all the past and all the future, could tell him what he must do to lift this curse from Thebes.

As he lashed the horses through the main gates and out on to the road, Laius remembered, with a shudder, the last time he had consulted the oracle many years before. Then, the priestess had told him he would be killed by his own son. Laius had at once abandoned the baby prince on the mountainside and left him to the jackals. "What horrors might the oracle have in store for me this time?" he wondered.

He drove on, heading for the narrow pass between the mountains that was the only safe route out of Thebes.

While Laius was heading towards the pass that would take him to the oracle, a weary traveller was just entering the pass in order to reach the besieged city. Oedipus, adopted son of the king and queen of Corinth, had just consulted the oracle, and had received a terrifying message.

"You will kill your father and marry your mother," the priestess had told him.

Oedipus dared not return home to Corinth. He loved King Polybus and Queen Periboea, his adopted parents. He couldn't imagine how he might end up killing his father and marrying his mother, but everybody knew that the oracle was always right. Rather than take the risk he had decided to run away – as far and as fast as he could. Thebes would be his first stop, and then … he didn't know. But anything was better than what the oracle had foretold.

Oedipus looked down the long canyon that led to the city. In the distance, he could see a cloud of dust coming towards him. Warily, Oedipus drew his sword. He had heard rumours of the beast that preyed on travellers to Thebes, that was why he was taking this route and not going by the main road over the mountains.

With relief, he realised it was only a chariot, speeding towards him. Oedipus sheathed his sword and continued to walk along the narrow track.

As the chariot sped down the canyon, Laius whipped on the horses once again. Laius' breathing was fast and shallow. He had always hated enclosed spaces, and the steep, rocky walls seemed to be pressing in on him, toppling forward to crush him.

He lashed the horses on furiously. The poor animals pulled forwards frantically against their harnesses, trying to get away from the sharp, searing pain that cut into their backs and flanks.

Laius looked ahead and saw a traveller walking along the narrow path towards them.

"Sound the signal," he commanded the guards. "Make him stand aside."

One of the guards lifted a curved bronze trumpet to his lips and blew three long, deep blasts.

The distant stranger looked up, but continued walking.

"Insolent dog!" bellowed Laius. "Doesn't he know that he must show respect – that I am the king! Sound the signal again!"

Once again three trumpet blasts echoed along the canyon. Once again the traveller looked up, but continued walking towards the onrushing chariot.

As they drew level with the stranger, Laius reined in the horses and brought the chariot to a halt.

"You!' he bellowed. "Who do you think you are – not to step aside when commanded to by your betters?"

Oedipus looked all around. "My betters?" he said quietly, as if puzzled. "I see no one here who is better than me. All I see is an ill-bred, ill-mannered lout and two armed thugs! You may be sure that as I soon as I meet my *betters* I will step aside as you suggest."

Turning his back on the chariot, Oedipus once again began his long walk to Thebes.

"You two!" Laius screamed at his guards. "Get him! Show him how we reward such insolence!"

The two guards jumped from the chariot, but Oedipus had already spun round, sword in hand. As the two guards rushed at him, Oedipus whirled his sword in a gleaming figure of eight and cut down both men. Then, sword in hand, he approached the chariot and Laius.

"So, you are brave enough to give orders to your hired bully boys," sneered Oedipus, "but are you brave enough to fight your own battles?"

Laius hauled at the bridles of the two horses and lashed out with his whip to try and make the horses charge down Oedipus. But the horses had suffered enough. Instead of leaping forward they reared, throwing Laius out of the chariot and on to the drawn sword of Oedipus.

Oedipus rolled the richly dressed body off him and clambered to his feet. Three corpses lay on the path. In the distance he could see the horses bolting back to Thebes, dragging the empty chariot behind them.

Oedipus was stunned. All he had been doing was walking peacefully down a road. Through no fault that he could see, he was now the killer of a rich man and his two armed servants.

"They'll send a search party out," Oedipus muttered to himself. "I'd better take another route into Thebes – unless I want to stand trial for murder!"

He scanned the cliff sides. A few metres further on was a thin watercourse cut into the soft, dusty rock.

Oedipus scrambled up the gully until he reached the cliff top, then began the long walk up the side of Mount Phicium.

The Sphinx was sunning herself on a rock, trying to ignore the empty rumbling in her belly. It had been two days since the last traveller had come across the mountain and stayed for dinner. The Sphinx was getting very hungry and very bad-tempered.

Then she heard the sound of footsteps. She sat upright on the rock. A traveller was coming. She licked her lips.

Oedipus clambered up the mountainside, around a large grey boulder – and came face to face with the Sphinx.

"Good day," purred the Sphinx.

"Good day to you," replied Oedipus, without hesitating.

"Well, well," said the Sphinx admiringly, "someone with a little courage – and manners. Most men are too cowardly or rude – I'm never sure which – to respond politely to my greeting. Are you not afraid?"

"Of what should I be afraid?" asked Oedipus.

"Good chap!" said the Sphinx. "A worthy adversary at last! I am the Sphinx, and I like games. Do you like games?"

Oedipus shrugged. "Some I like, some I don't."

"This is my favourite game," announced the Sphinx. "I ask you a riddle … you get it wrong … I eat you up."

"A riddle?" said Oedipus thoughtfully. "But what if I get it right?"

"Don't worry about that," said the Sphinx. "No one ever does. And I have a very special riddle for you, my brave little man; one I have been saving for a truly worthy opponent. *What creature has four legs in the morning, two legs at noon and three at evening?*"

"Oh, that's easy!" replied Oedipus. "A man."

"*What?*" shrieked the Sphinx.

"A man," repeated Oedipus. "In the morning of his life – when he is a baby – he crawls on four legs. When he is grown, he walks upright on two. When he is old – in the evening of his life – he walks with a stick: three legs."

With an awful howl, the Sphinx beat her enormous wings and rose into the air.

"You have destroyed me!" she screamed. "I am doomed … but you, you are doomed as well. Remember me, and in the years to come you will wish that you had died here on this mountainside and not I!"

With a final scream she folded her wings, plunged over the precipice and smashed herself to pieces on the rocks way down in the barren valley below.

THE LAIDLY WORM

THE LAIDLY WORM

Long ago, in Bamburgh Castle, in the borderlands north of the river Tyne, there lived a king and queen. They had a son and heir, who was called Childe Wynd, and a daughter, who was named Margaret.

When the king first ruled the land, there were many wars against the wild northern tribes who would swarm over the great wall which – some said – giants had built many centuries before. As the years went on, the king brought peace to the land, for he was both a great warrior and a maker of good laws which all of his people respected and obeyed. Just when lasting peace seemed to have come to the kingdom, the queen became ill and died.

The loss of his queen nearly broke the king's heart. Overnight, it seemed, he changed from a brave warrior with a mighty, rumbling laugh to a stooped, old man. He shuffled through the empty, echoing corridors of his castle, unshaved and unwashed, dressed in a coarse, woollen robe that even the humblest monk would have thrown out.

For a year and a day the castle was kept in the deepest mourning. Heavy black curtains hung at every window to keep out the daylight, and all the mirrors were shrouded with black veils. All banquets and feasts were stopped, and the king and his family and all their courtiers ate only bread, water and boiled root vegetables – food that even the humblest peasant would have refused.

So deep and despairing was the sorrow of the king, that his people began to whisper amongst themselves. "This is more than just grief; the king has been cursed. He has become an old man. What if the wild tribes of the north should come? There is no one to protect us."

As the king sickened, so did his people and their land. It was as if hope itself had been banished. The crops rotted, unharvested, in the fields; the pigs and cattle, sickened by neglect, died in the fields. It was indeed as if the land had been cursed.

It didn't take long before some of the people began to whisper that perhaps it was time to throw off the priests and return to the ancient ways. The king should make the age-old sacrifice, they said: lay down his life that the land might become fertile again!

Childe Wynd heard the rumours and whispers. "Someone has to act," he thought. "My father can do nothing; it is up to me now as the heir to the throne."

Childe Wynd went searching for his father. He found the king in the highest tower room of the castle. There was no furniture in the room, just filthy straw on the floor. The king was sitting in the middle of the room, motionless, staring into midair.

"Father," said Childe Wynd. "I beg permission to go on crusade to the Holy Land. The fields are barren and the people are in despair. Maybe it is true we are accursed or bewitched. But maybe, if I go on crusade, this curse will be lifted."

"Do as you please, my boy," the king replied, with a weary sigh. "Nothing will lift the curse on me, for nothing will bring your mother back. Go if you must ... but leave me in peace –

here with my grief."

So Childe Wynd set off for the Holy Land. He knew enough of the Old Ways to make sure that the ship he sailed in had a keel made of rowan wood (because the old, wise ones said that rowan wood would repel evil and witchcraft), and he carried to the wars a spear whose shaft was cut from the branch of a rowan tree.

Three weeks after Childe Wynd had left for the wars, a miracle occurred – or so it seemed at the time – the king fell in love! Hopelessly, insanely in love, as if he had been enchanted or bewitched.

He had left his tower room, and was wandering in the thick woods that surrounded the castle, when he saw a woman dressed in green walking through the trees a little way ahead of him. She turned and smiled at him. The king gasped at her beauty; and as he gazed at her, the memories of the queen, his wife, began to fade away. In place of his grief, the king now felt an irresistible urge to be with this strange woman – to gaze at her, to adore her, to worship her. All other thoughts and feelings disappeared like mist rising from a lake and melting into the morning air.

Back at the castle, day turned to night and night to day again and still the king didn't return. For six days the king was gone, without a word of explanation. Then, on the seventh day, he returned.

Margaret rushed to him and threw her arms round his neck. "Oh, father! Father! Where have you been? I have been so worried! Seven days without a word!"

The king brushed her aside. A strange, cold, faraway light was in his eyes. "Nonsense, child!" he replied. "I have been gone but one day. Enough of your prattling. Greet your new mother!"

The king gestured behind him, and Margaret saw for the first time the green-cloaked woman of the woods. The two women stared at each other. Margaret gazed in astonishment; the new queen gazed at Margaret with hatred. In the years since her mother's death, Margaret had grown into a beautiful, young woman. "A rival – and a mortal one, too!" thought the new queen. "Just wait, my pretty. Have I got a surprise in store for you!"

That night, when everyone in the castle was asleep, the new queen rose from her bed and tiptoed down the deserted corridor to the room where Margaret slept. Silently opening the great oak door, she crept in.

Three times the wicked queen walked round the bed on which Margaret slept; three times she passed her hands above the body of the sleeping princess; three times she whispered strange words in the young woman's ear. As the wicked queen slipped silently out of the door, the room slowly began to fill with thick, acrid smoke.

Soon all the corridors and passageways were filled with the stinking smog. Guards and servants woke choking in their beds. From all over the castle people ran to find out where the fire – for that is what they assumed – had broken out.

As they reached the royal bedrooms, they were faced with a horrifying sight. Blocking the corridor was an enormous creature that looked something like a slowworm, except that it was covered in slime like a slug. As the servants shrank back, screaming and retching, the horrible creature oozed its way down the passage, across the great hall and out of the main gate of the castle.

The Captain of the guard called the roll: all his soldiers were accounted for. The Chamberlain checked off all the servants: none missing. It was only when everyone was going back to bed that one of the kitchen boys asked: "Where is her Royal Highness, the Princess Margaret?"

The castle was searched and searched again, from the highest tower room to the deepest cellar, but no trace of the beautiful princess could be found. There was no one in the castle so simple that they didn't realise at once what had happened: the hideous creature had devoured the princess!

For seven days and seven nights the creature terrorised the countryside around the castle, devouring everything and everyone it met. Then at the end of its seventh night, the worm coiled itself around the highest hill, Spindlestone Heugh, to rest after its gluttony.

Anyone brave enough – or stupid enough – to creep up Spindlestone Heugh would have seen that the great worm's slime-covered body shook with sobs, and huge tears welled up from its dead, black eyes.

"It is a creature of the devil sent by God to punish you for your sins!" boomed the bishop.

"What sins have I committed that have not already been punished enough?" asked the king. "My first queen and my daughter both dead; and my new queen has vanished – no trace of her has been seen for days. Tell me, priest, for I do not know: what sin could I have committed so great that I should be so tormented but of which I have no memory?"

"Pride! Anger! Gluttony!" yelled the bishop, his mad eyes gleaming. "Avarice! Envy! Sloth! White spittle appeared at the corner of his mouth. "Lechery!" he screamed. "Man wallows in a stinking cess-pit of sin! There is sin everywhere! Everywhere the stench and filth! Everywhere – "

"Guards!" yelled the king. "Take the bishop away and lock him in his church until he calms down!"

The shrieking prelate was dragged from the hall.

The bishop and his priests could offer nothing but sermons. Such a beast as the worm of Spindlestone Heugh could not be preached away, the king knew that. With a shudder, he decided that it was time to consult older, darker forces.

The king squatted down in the mouth of the cave and watched as a frail old man hung a blackened pot over the fire and began to stir.

"I must warn your majesty that the Sight may not come to me," said the old man. "The Goddess should be served by a priestess ... but we have had none for so many generations." He sighed and shrugged his shoulders.

The pot began to bubble. A strange, sharp fragrance rose into the cool night air. The old man bent his head over the pot and inhaled the vapours – once, twice, three times. Then he sat opposite the king with his eyes closed.

The king waited – five minutes, ten minutes, fifteen minutes. He sighed. He could guess what would happen next. The old man would go into a trance, then he would make strange noises, talk gibberish for ten minutes, and finally demand an enormous fee.

The old man's eyes suddenly snapped open. His eyes were clear and bright and his voice firmer and deeper than it had been. "This creature was not created by either your God or your

Devil," he told the king. "It was made by one who was old when the world was new – the one who was your queen, but is now gone back to her own country. She may return, but she may not. Pray to your God she does not. Your daughter Margaret is alive, but that is all I know. She has been hidden, but I don't know where."

"But what can I do to get rid of the worm?" asked the king, eager to know more.

"Only one of your blood can destroy the worm," said the old man. "But neither you nor your daughter can do anything, for you have both taken food from the woman in green. Only your son, Childe Wynd, can destroy it."

"But he is far away, on crusade," groaned the king.

"He will be here in seven days, with a fair wind from France," said the old man. "He has been travelling homeward for many weary months."

"Is there nothing to be done about the worm until he returns?" asked the king. "In seven days the worm could destroy half the kingdom."

"Yes," said the old man. "Set aside seven cows. Milk them each evening, then at nightfall take the milk to Spindlestone Heugh. At the foot of the Heugh you will find a stone trough, carved out of the living rock and almost as old as the Heugh itself. Fill it with the milk of the seven cows. The worm will feed on that, then it will sleep until the next evening when you must feed it in the same manner again. That way your lands and your people will be safe."

"Thank you," said the king, sincerely. "What reward can I give you?"

"No gifts," said the old man, proudly. "I am no conjuror. But

one thing you can give me: your protection from the priests. I fear those grey men and their evil fires."

The screaming wind whipped the sea into a cauldron of boiling foam round the tiny ship. Rain lashed the deck as Childe Wynd peered towards the shore. Soon they would round the headland and reach the shelter of the tiny harbour.

Childe Wynd raised a hand to his brow to keep the rain out of his eyes and peered harder. He was sure he had seen a figure on the cliffs, a woman dressed in a long green robe who was waving her arms as if she was urging on the storm. Once again Childe Wynd gave thanks for the rowan keel beneath the ship.

As the ship sailed past the grey cliffs and towards the port, the storm stopped instantly. Astonished, the sailors gazed at the flat, calm sea all around them.

The ship inched its way along the small stone quay. At the far end of the quay stood the king. The Childe Wynd leapt from the ship and ran to embrace his father.

"My boy, I must talk to you of dreadful things," said the king, as soon as they were safely back in Bamburgh Castle. "Such suffering we have had! Your sister has disappeared, and a dreadful serpent threatens the kingdom. Even now it is coiled around Spindlestone Heugh, and only you can destroy it."

Childe Wynd crept up the hill towards the coiled worm. In his hand was the rowan wood spear. He would kill the worm before it could wake.

Childe Wynd stood beside the enormous head of the beast, and raised his spear high … and …

"Oh, Childe Wynd," sighed the creature in a voice Childe

Wynd knew well. "You have come to release me from this hideous curse. Oh, Childe Wynd, my brother!"

"Margaret!" gasped Childe Wynd in amazement. "What must I do?"

"Kiss me," said the hideous creature. "Three times."

Childe Wynd did not put down his spear. "This could be a trap to enchant me," he thought. He leant forward and kissed the beast's cheek. The stench that came from the creature drove the air from Childe Wynd's lungs and made him choke.

"Again," whispered the sweet voice.

Childe Wynd pressed his lips to the monster's cheek. This time slime coated his face. He began to retch.

"Courage, my brother," came Margaret's voice again. "Just one more kiss."

Childe Wynd closed his eyes and swallowing hard to control his nausea, he kissed the creature again.

He opened his eyes, and there stood his sister, Margaret, dressed once again in her nightgown. Before they could say a word to each other, there came a dreadful shriek from behind them. "You will not beat me so easily, Childe Wynd!"

Childe Wynd turned to face the wizened hag dressed all in green. As she raised her hand, he lashed out with his spear. The point of the spear did not touch her, but as the rowan wood shaft smacked into the wicked queen's forehead, her body started to shrivel. She began to collapse into herself like a punctured balloon. A foul smell rose into the air, and where a woman had once stood there was now nothing but an ugly toad.

I would like to tell you that they all lived happily ever after. But they didn't. Not that they were particularly unhappy either. The king and his children lived on at Bamburgh and did their best to rule their people fairly. Sometimes they succeeded, sometimes they didn't. Although they went to church every Sunday to hear the bishop preach his sermons, above the throne in the great hall hung the rowan keel from Childe Wynd's ship. From that day on Childe Wynd never let go of his rowan wood spear. For, although they were a pious family, their sufferings had made them wise.

BEOWULF AND GRENDEL

BEOWULF AND GRENDEL

Long ago the great warlord Hrothgar
Built a mighty hall he called Heorot,
A house far greater than men on earth
Had ever dreamed of before.
There he would share with all his people
The gifts which God bestowed upon him.
There they would feast, and while they feasted
Hrothgar would give them jewelled rings –
Magnificent gifts from his battle-treasure.
Boldly the hall stood, and every night
The walls would ring with shouts and laughter
As the mightiest warriors, lords and princes
Feasted with Hrothgar the king.

But beyond the lights that blazed at the banquet
There dwelt in the depths of the outer darkness
One who heard the hall filled with laughter,
Who heard each night the joy of the feasting,
Who heard the sounds of the harp and the singing
And felt only pain and was gnawed by hatred.
Unknowing, believing that all was well,
The men of Heorot had awoken one
Who held in himself all the ancient evil:

Grendel, who haunted the stinking marshes,
Whose home was the fen and the barren rocks;
Grendel, cast out by God himself
Into the land of monstrous beings;
Banished in torment far from humankind –
Grendel: every man's deepest nightmare.

With the falling of night came the horror of Grendel,
Came to Heorot, burst into the hall,
Found Hrothgar's warriors peacefully sleeping
(After the banquet had finally ended).
In rage and in fury this child of evil
Tore from their beds thirty warriors;
In hunger he slaughtered them, carried them home
And on warriors' blood did Grendel feast.

Night after night Grendel returned
Until no one dared to sleep at Heorot.
Grendel, in all his power and fury,
He was the Lord of Heorot now.
In the black, fearful nights in Heorot he camped
Where the stench of the slaughterhouse clung to the walls;
While the people of Heorot prayed to their gods
For an end to their misery.

And for a time their prayers seemed fully answered:
To Heorot came a kinsman of the king,
The hero Beowulf, who swore to destroy
That vile, night-stalking fiend.
Secretly a trap was set for Grendel –

Grendel came stalking up from the marshes,
Up from the moors he came dragging the mists:
Grendel, the bearer of God's deepest wrath,
The sorrow of women, the anger of men.
Grendel came onwards, then stopped.
At the door he could smell the fresh scent of man,
And the door was shut tightly and bolted against him!

Grendel tore the door asunder,
Maddened frenzy drove him onwards,
The vile light of all his sickness
Burned like plague with his eyes.
He saw the warriors, thought them sleeping,
Knew them for a source of food.
Seizing one in taloned fingers
Killed it; but still filled with hunger,
Out stretched Grendel's hand again
To grab another.

Then Grendel felt something he'd never felt before;
He who had brought fear to so many
Now felt fear of his own.
A hand as mighty as his
Had grasped him in the darkness.
In that foul pit of Grendel's mind
Where he could think and feel,
Fear took the place of rage, pain and vengeance –
All Grendel's power, his strength
Directed to escape, to flee back

To his vile home in the marshes, away
From that strong hand that seized him in the dark.

Howled and shrieked and battled Grendel,
Fear and fierceness drove him onwards:
Fast held the hand of darkness on his arm.
The walls of Heorot echoed Grendel's cries;
Crashing over through the wreck of Heorot,
Grendel and his foe fought to the death.

The warriors lay blinded by the dark,
Powerless. They could hear the sounds of battle –
Then came a shriek, a dreadful tearing sound
And through the door the scream of some wild beast
Its death wound suffered, howling home to die.

And in their midst stood Beowulf, triumphant;
The arm of Grendel torn from out his shoulder
Held aloft in Beowulf's unbroken grasp.

THE CYCLOPES

THE CYCLOPES

When the great war at Troy had ended, and the Greek army had turned the once magnificent city into nothing but a heap of rubble and smouldering cinders, the Greek kings and their soldiers left the defeated Trojans, returned to their ships and sailed home. The lucky ones were back in their homes within a week, because the distance between the coast of Turkey – where the city of Troy stood – and Greece is not great. Some were unlucky and sailed into storms and were blown many miles off-course, or became becalmed and had to row all the way home; they may have taken two or three weeks to get home. Odysseus, King of Ithaca, took *twenty years* to get home.

For twenty years Odysseus and his companions were lashed by hurricanes and typhoons, sucked into whirlpools, crushed by rocks, enchanted by witches and sirens, and had to fight more monsters and terrifying beasts than you would imagine existed. This is the story of one of those battles: how Odysseus and his friends escaped from the dreadful, one-eyed giant, Polyphemus the cyclopes.

Many weary months had passed since the little ship had left the coast of Troy. Odysseus and his men had become separated from the rest of the fleet in a great storm. Their ship had then been blown on to the coast of North Africa. Now, at last, they were sailing north again towards Ithaca.

As daylight dawned, Odysseus began his inspection of the

ship's stores. It was worse than he had feared. They were getting low on food, he had realised that already. What he hadn't realised was that one of the water barrels had been leaking. With luck, their fresh water might last them two days, but no more. They would have to risk going ashore once more to take on more water and more food.

With barely a grunt to the men on early watch, Odysseus returned to his place in the stern of the boat and unwrapped his charts from their cover of oiled cloth. He peered at the faded diagrams, then he carefully traced a line with his finger across the map: Sicily. They could land on the island of Sicily to take on fresh supplies.

He re-wrapped the primitive charts and tucked them safely in their hiding place between the lining boards in the side of the boat. The men were still in awe of the way Odysseus seemed to know – even after a storm – where they were. They didn't know about the charts and probably wouldn't have understood them if they did. "It is good for a king to appear to have a few mysterious powers," thought Odysseus, as he clambered back towards the prow to look out for the coast of Sicily.

Late that afternoon they dropped anchor in a small, rocky cove. Daylight was fading as they waded ashore. In front of them was a narrow path that wound up the steep cliffs that encircled the tiny bay, and halfway up the path was the entrance to a cave.

"Wait here," Odysseus commanded his men. "I think I can see a place where we can spend the night, but I want to make sure it's safe."

Drawing his sword, Odysseus crept up the path to the mouth of the cave. He peered inside. He couldn't see any signs of anyone living in the cave. He sniffed. there was a slight scent of some animal – sheep, maybe; goat more likely – but there wasn't the heavy, musky smell of bear or the acrid stink of mountain lion.

Odysseus came out of the cave and looked round the hillside. In the distance, he could see a couple of goats cropping the coarse grass. He smiled to himself; he had been right about the smell.

Within an hour, Odysseus and his crew had made themselves as comfortable as possible in the cave. They had lit a fire, and the air was now scented with the fragrance of roasting goat meat.

Suddenly, the cave was plunged into complete darkness. Someone or something had completely blocked the entrance and shut out the twilight.

Odysseus' eyes quickly grew used to the sudden darkness. He looked towards the cave mouth and gasped. Standing in the entrance was a giant, at least four metres tall, with one huge eye in the middle of his forehead.

"I am Polyphemus," boomed the giant, "king of the Cyclopes. Who dares to enter my cave, and steal and kill my goats? Step forward and show yourself!"

Brave as he was, Odysseus could not stop his legs trembling as he walked forward to the centre of the cave. He bowed low.

"Please forgive us, my noble lord Polyphemus. We had no idea that you lived in this cave, or that the goats we killed were anything but wild creatures belonging to no one. I beg you, please accept our most humble apologies."

Polyphemus snatched up Odysseus between his thumb and forefinger. The enormous creature's manner changed immediately. A soppy grin came on to his face. His voice went high and lispy, like an enormous toddler's.

"Ooooh looky – a talking dolly! A teensy-weensy human. I like ickle, teensy humans. Do you know what I do with teensy-weensy humans?"

He paused. Odysseus was too terrified to answer.

"No? Well I'll tell you," the cyclopes continued, in his soppy voice. "I play with them for a week or two until I get bored, then . . ." His voice returned to its normal deafening boom: "I pull their arms and legs off and I eat them!"

He stared down at Odysseus. "I think I'll call you Tiddleypush, or Rinky-dink, because you're so tiddly and dinky," he continued in his babyish voice.

All the time the cyclopes had been talking, Odysseus had been desperately trying to think of a plan. The glimmer of an idea had begun to form.

"Oh, mighty Polyphemus," he began in as brave a voice as he could manage. "Those are splendid names – absolutely delightful names, and you must be very clever indeed to think them up. But I will tell you my real name, if you wish: it is *No-Man.*"

"No-Man?" repeated Polyphemus. "That's a strange name – but I like it. Right, I will call you No-Man – until I get bored with you, then I will call you Dinner-Man." And he laughed heartily at his own joke. "But now is not the time to play with you," said the cyclopes, putting Odysseus back on the ground. "I must go and bring in my flock for the night."

The cyclopes strode towards the mouth of the cave. "Don't run away," he said. "I'll be back later to play with you and your tiny friends."

With that he left the cave, sliding an enormous boulder over
the entrance. Odysseus and his men rushed forward and pushed
with all their strength against the boulder, but they could not
move it one centimetre.

"Search the cave," Odysseus ordered, "and quickly! See if
there's anything we could use as a lever."

"Here!" yelled one of the sailors. "It's an enormous pole, or
staff – or something. I can't move it on my own."

Together, the ship's crew manoeuvred the enormous pole
into a narrow gap beneath the boulder and heaved with all their
might. The boulder didn't move, but with a loud crack, the end
of the pole split off and Odysseus and his men tumbled on to
the earth floor of the cave.

"What do we do now?" groaned one of the sailors in despair.

Odysseus felt the bottom of the pole to see what damage had
been done. The jagged end was as sharp as a spear.

"I know!" he exclaimed. "Carry it over to the fire, and hold
the broken end in the fire – not enough to burn it, but enough
to harden it. Then hide it in the back of the cave. But in the name
of Zeus be quick! That ghastly creature will be back soon … "

It was some hours before Polyphemus returned. He rounded up
his goats and counted them. One of the goats was missing. He
counted them again to make sure. Yes, one was definitely
missing. He set off across the hills to find his missing goat. It was
only after he'd been searching for two hours that he
remembered the tiny men had killed and cooked one of his
goats. By the time he returned to the cave he was exhausted and
in a very bad mood.

He rolled back the enormous rock, shooed the goats into the cave, and rolled the rock back again.

"No-Man!" he boomed. "Tomorrow we will play. We will play a game called *Punishment.* I will punish you for killing my goat. I will drop you on to the floor of the cave until you scream for mercy, then I will pull off your arms and legs, and eat you for my breakfast. Goodnight! Sleep well!"

Odysseus and his men waited until the giant's breathing became heavy and deep. As soon as he began to snore Odysseus spoke to the huddle of frightened men. "Do not fear," he whispered. "I know how to get us out of here, but we must wait until it is nearly morning. Then, when I give the order, you must each grab a goat. Climb underneath it, clinging on to the fur. If you do as I say we will be gone by first light tomorrow, I promise you."

Odysseus and his men lay awake, but silent, for one hour … two … three … four. At the start of the fifth hour, Odysseus crept to the back of the cave and dragged out the sharpened pole.

He returned to his men. "Now!" he whispered. As each man selected a goat, Odysseus crept forward to where Polyphemus was sleeping. Using all his strength, he raised high the stake and plunged it into the sleeping cyclopes' single eye.

With a tremendous scream, Polyphemus awoke. "Help me! Help me!" he yelled. "Someone, please help me!"

The ground shook as the other cyclopes, awoken by Polyphemus' cries, ran to the cave.

"Polyphemus! What's wrong?" they called. "What's the matter? Why are you screaming?"

"It is No-Man!" howled Polyphemus. "No-Man is hurting me!

No-Man has blinded me!"

The other cyclopes laughed. "Go back to sleep then," they said. "You've been having a nightmare. Just as long as no man is hurting you, you'll be quite safe!"

Despite Polyphemus' begging and pleading, the other cyclopes went back to bed.

Polyphemus crawled to the cave mouth, moaning in agony. He pushed the great boulder aside, but the other cyclopes had gone.

Odysseus climbed beneath the last goat and slapped it on the flank. The goat trotted forward. Polyphemus, hearing a noise behind him, called out: "Who's there?"

There was no answer. He groped blindly round, but touching the rough hair on the goat's back he let it trot out of the cave entrance. One by one, the goats walked past Polyphemus. Each time he reached out and felt the goat's back to make sure that it wasn't that dreadful No-Man or his companions getting away; and each time he was satisfied that it wasn't.

Once safely away from the cave, Odysseus and each of his crew members dropped to the ground, and then crept silently down the slope to where their ship was lying at anchor.

THE MINOTAUR

THE MINOTAUR

Throughout the ancient world the city state of Athens was famous for the wisdom of its great thinkers, for the wonderful stories and plays which were composed by its poets, and for the brilliance of its engineers and inventors. In the same way, Sparta was renowned for its fierce warriors. But for many years, the most powerful state of all was – and you may be surprised to learn this – the island of Crete. And the most powerful king in the ancient world was the king of Crete, Minos.

If you look carefully at a map of the Mediterranean Sea you will see why. In between Greece and Turkey and the rich grain lands of North Africa (as they were in those days) – like a spider squatting in the middle of a web – sat the island of Crete, ruled by King Minos. His fleets of pirate ships were the terror of the Mediterranean. No one could carry a cargo of corn or oil or wine across the sea without being stopped by one of Minos' ships. Every town, every city had to pay Minos' hired thugs, or their ships and cargoes would be stolen and their citizens would go hungry. Nowadays we would call that a "protection racket" or "blackmail", or in simple plain English: "theft". Minos called it "tribute".

"After all," he would say, "I am the most powerful king in the world. And I deserve *respect!*"

But Minos knew deep down – for whatever else he might have been he was not a stupid man – that no one really respected him. For hour after hour he sat alone in his dark, gloomy throne room in the centre of his palace at Knossos, like the spider at the centre of its web, brooding on what other people thought of him. Everyone he could think of feared him. His palace guards feared him; the toughest of his sea-captains feared him; even his daughter, Ariadne, feared him. But who truly respected him? Who loved him – in the way that old Aegeus, king of Athens, was loved by *his* people? No one.

Minos sat alone in his throne room for days and weeks and months, as his "tributes" piled up in his grain stores and his wine cellars; as the sacks of gold filled up one treasure room after another; and slowly but surely King Minos went mad.

In the middle of the night, King Minos emerged from his isolation and called his ministers together. He had worked out a plan to make himself the most feared and respected king that had ever lived – or would ever live.

"Who is the most feared king in all the world?" demanded King Minos.

"Y – you are, y – your majesty," chorused all the ministers together. King Minos could tell by the way their knees were knocking together under their nightgowns that they were telling the truth.

"And who is the best loved king in all the world?" Minos demanded, his mad eyes shining in the flickering lamplight.

"Er … y – you are, your m – magnificence."

This time the king could tell by the way their knees were knocking together underneath their nightgowns that his ministers were *not* telling the truth. He decided to ignore it for the moment.

"Good, good – well answered," said the king. "I have a plan – a brilliant plan. There is, I have heard, in the furthest corner of this island the most fearful monster that has ever fed on human flesh. It is half giant, half bull. I have ordered my guards to capture it and bring it here, to Knossos. As a special honour to the creature, I have decided to name it after me: Minotaur. It will make me the most feared and respected king that has ever lived, or ever will live! Now, answer me truthfully: who is the most brilliant inventor and engineer in the world?"

The ministers looked at each other, appalled. They had never been asked that question before.

"Y – y – you are, your ma – " they started to chant.

"No, no, NO!" bellowed King Minos, punching his forehead in exasperation. "I said: answer me *truthfully!*"

There was a long pause. Then a voice from the back stammered: "I – if you p – please, y – your majesty – I have heard that Daedalus the Athenian is the cleverest man."

"At last!" groaned the king. "Well answered. There is a ship waiting in the harbour. Go at once and don't come back without Daedalus. I have a very special job for him. Agree to pay him anything he asks. Well? What are you waiting for? GO!"

A year later, King Aegeus was sitting in the great hall of his palace in Athens listening to his son, Theseus. Theseus was telling his father all about his latest victory at a wrestling match. What Theseus was actually saying was mind-numbingly boring, but Aegeus didn't mind. For the last twenty years Theseus had lived with his mother, many miles away.

It was a joy for Aegeus just to sit and gaze at the lad. He was quite a sight, too. Two metres tall, as muscular as Hercules, long flowing blonde hair, blue eyes and a voice as sweet as Apollo's, the god of music and poetry. Aegeus couldn't work out where

Theseus had got his extraordinary good looks from. It certainly wasn't from him, and as far as he could remember it couldn't have been from his mother either.

" … so then, in round seven, I thought to myself: 'Theseus, it's time to stop being Mr Nice Guy.' So I grabbed him round the waist, got him into the Spartan stranglehold, then as soon as he started gasping for mercy I turned him upside down – and wham! I pile-drivered him into the floor! He was deader than a Saturday night in Hades! Laugh? I nearly died!"

"Your majesty, excuse me." It was the chief minister. "The Cretan ambassador is outside. He says it is an urgent matter … "

"Anyway, like I was saying," continued Theseus, "Demeter was there – you know, Zeus' sister – and she said to me: 'I haven't seen pectorals like yours since – ' "

"Later, my boy, later," said Aegeus. "I fear this may be a very grave matter."

"Your majesty," said the ambassador, bowing low in front of the throne. "I come here to arrange for you to pay tribute to my sovereign lord, King Minos."

"But we paid last month – " began King Aegeus.

"A *new* tribute," continued the ambassador. "Seven young men and seven maidens."

"Why?" asked the king. "What does he want them for?"

"Your majesty has doubtless heard of the dreadful Minotaur," said the ambassador, in his most sinisterly silky voice.

The old king shuddered.

"King Minos requires them to feed the Minotaur," explained the ambassador.

"No!" protested Aegeus. "I could never agree to such a tribute."

"It's the usual arrangement," continued the ambassador, unimpressed. "You pay the tribute, or Athens starves. Sparta and Thebes have already paid, so now it is your turn. His majesty King Minos has most kindly provided a ship, which is anchored in your harbour. You can't miss it: it has black sails – a most fitting gesture, don't you think?"

"No! It's barbaric! It's unthinkable!"

"I would think about it if I were you," said the ambassador, turning towards the door. "Think about the women and children of Athens dying of starvation. Let me put it this way: King Minos has just made you an offer you can't refuse!" Bowing one last time, the Cretan ambassador swept out of the room.

"Don't worry, father," said Theseus, as soon as they were alone. "I'll go and I'll kill the Minotaur!"

"But my boy – " began Aegeus.

"Bulls are nothing," said Theseus, sweeping his majestic golden locks off his forehead. "I've wrestled bulls before. All you have to do is grab them round the neck in a Spartan stranglehold, wait until they go dizzy, and then bang their heads on the ground. It's easy!"

Spiros sat in the prow of the black-sailed ship, feeling miserable. As if being fed to a hideous monster wasn't bad enough, since they had set sail his fiancée, Helena, could hardly find the time to exchange two words with him. Like every other girl on the ship, she seemed to be head over heels in love with Prince Theseus.

He heard a light footstep on the planking. He looked up. At last: Helena.

"Why are you moping around up here?" she asked. "You're

being boring, and Theseus doesn't like people who are boring. And don't look so miserable. Theseus will kill the monster – he's promised!"

"Hmmmph!" replied Spiros, sulkily.

"You're just jealous because Theseus is so good-looking, and tall, and rich, and has such gorgeous muscles!"

"Hmmmmph!" replied Spiros again. It was difficult to argue; who *wouldn't* be jealous of someone who had all that?

Theseus' beautiful voice drifted along the boat to where they were sitting. " ... as I told my father, King Aegeus, as soon as I've killed the Minotaur I'll take down the black sails and put on white, and then it's all back to the palace for the biggest party Athens has ever seen."

"Land-ho!" Theseus was interrupted by the cry from the sailor at the top of the mast.

"Good-oh!" exclaimed Theseus. "I've just got time to practise the Spartan stranglehold once more before we land. Where's Spiros?"

"Oh no!" groaned Spiros.

"Coward!" taunted Helena.

"Hmmmmph!" replied Spiros. He couldn't argue with that, either.

As soon as she saw the tall, muscular, blond Athenian come ashore, Ariadne, princess of Crete, felt her knees knocking together and her stomach go into knots. What was this strange feeling? Her knees often knocked together when she was summoned by her father, but the feeling she felt now wasn't fear. "Could it be love?" she wondered. She didn't know; but what she did know was that she couldn't *bear* to think of this beautiful youth being devoured by that fearful monster.

But how could he be saved? The monster lived at the centre of the Labyrinth – the most complicated maze in the world – built by Daedalus on her father's orders. The "tributes" were permitted no weapons when they entered the Labyrinth. Even if – and this was most unlikely – someone could kill the creature with his bare hands, they would never be able to find their way out of the Labyrinth again.

Only one man knew the way in and out of the Labyrinth: Daedalus. Would he help? After all, he was an Athenian. Ariadne doubted it. If Daedalus had been a kindly man would he ever have agreed to build the Labyrinth in the first place?

She watched as the procession came slowly up the narrow path from the harbour. She noticed that the golden youth who made her heart pound and her head swim was leading the way. "Was he a rich man's son?" she wondered. He was certainly respected by the others.

A smaller man was walking behind the golden one. The smaller man was rubbing his neck as if it was bruised. As they drew level to Ariadne, she heard the small man say, "You may be a prince, Theseus, but that's no reason to go round dislocating other people's necks."

Theseus! Ariadne gasped. King Aegeus' son! Surely that might help persuade Daedalus to help her.

"Of *course* there's a way out," said Daedalus grumpily. "It's only a maze – it's not magic! But why should I help you save these people and risk my own neck?"

"But I wouldn't tell anyone," protested Ariadne.

"You wouldn't need to," sighed Daedalus. "Your father isn't

stupid. He'd soon work out who told them. You'd be above suspicion, and I'd be in the torture chamber!"

"But I'm going with them!" blurted out Ariadne. She hadn't known she was until she said it. "All the blame will fall on me."

"Hmmmm ... " Daedalus considered this information very carefully. "And who is this ... this creature you so adore that you're willing to give up everything for?"

"Theseus," replied Ariadne, blushing.

"Oh! Him!" exclaimed Daedalus. "I know Theseus, he's a second cousin on my mother's side. Beware of him. He may look gorgeous on the outside, but inside there's nothing. He'd make a wonderful statue, but a terrible husband. I'll help you, princess, but I warn you: *don't* fall in love with young Theseus!"

At first light next morning, Ariadne crept through the palace to the two rooms where the Athenians were sleeping. She tiptoed past the long line of beds until she saw Theseus' golden hair spread out on the pillow. She woke him as quietly as she could.

"I am Ariadne, daughter of King Minos," she whispered. "If you wish to kill the Minotaur and save yourself and your friends, follow me."

With a finger to her lips, she led Theseus along the deserted corridors, through a carved stone doorway, and out of the palace to the entrance of the Labyrinth.

"Why are you doing this?" asked Theseus.

All of a sudden, Ariadne's pent-up feelings came bursting out. Sobbing, she clung to his magnificently muscular chest.

"Oh, my darling, my darling!" she gasped. "Ever since I first saw you I knew I had to save you – I couldn't let you die! I don't know what's happening to me. All I know is that I want to spend the rest of my life with you. Do you think I'm totally mad? Please, my darling, say something. Give me a little hope that you might love me too … ."

"Err … well, um … yes." Theseus was embarrassed at this unexpected speech, but he was also shrewd enough to remember that she hadn't *actually* given him the secret of the Labyrinth yet. He cleared his throat.

"Why yes, of course. Give me the secret of the Labyrinth and I'll certainly … erm … I mean, I do – of course I do!"

"Do you really mean it?" asked Ariadne.

"Of course," replied Theseus, in his grandest, most prince-like voice. "Tell me what I have to do to kill the Minotaur, and I will gladly give you anything you ask."

"All I want is to be with you," gasped Ariadne, "for as long as you'll have me."

Theseus beamed his most gorgeous smile. "Give me the secret of the Labyrinth and we will be married as soon as we reach Athens!" he declared.

Theseus crept round the next corner of the Labyrinth. By the stench he could tell that he was getting close to the centre of the maze, where the Minotaur lived. With his hand he followed the thin thread of silk. That was the great secret that Daedalus had told Ariadne: tie one end of a ball of silk to the entrance and roll it into the Labyrinth. There was something about the slope of the floors that meant that the ball would roll to the middle. All he now had to do was follow the silk to the middle, then follow the silk out again. Easy! Certainly not a secret that was worth getting married for. Silly idea! Theseus was confident he would find a way of dumping her once they got back to Athens –

after all, he had managed to get rid of all his other fiancées easily enough, once they ceased to amuse him.

The other secret was a little more challenging, though. Ariadne had told him that the Minotaur could not be killed by any human-made weapon. Theseus flexed his biceps muscles. Don't worry, he said to himself, no one can beat me.

He crept forward, along the trail of silk.

Then all at once, with a deafening roar, the Minotaur was in front of him. Theseus stepped back in shock. The creature was enormous: three times the size of a normal bull, and standing erect on its back legs. Its horns jutted forward like … "Yes!" thought Theseus. "Like *spears*." He now knew how he was going to kill the creature.

The Minotaur circled his victim, snorting with rage. Then it lunged. Theseus sidestepped the charge, but as the Minotaur went past him, he grabbed its horn with both hands and wrenched. With the combined force of Theseus' strength and the Minotaur's own weight, there was a terrible cracking sound and the horn broke off in Theseus' hand.

The Minotaur let out a piercing, agonised scream. Blood flowed down its forehead into its eyes. Blindly it turned to charge again, but Theseus seized his moment. Stepping forward, he plunged the horn's point into the Minotaur's head. The monster fell dead at Theseus' feet.

Ariadne lifted her head up from Theseus' lap and gazed into his deep blue eyes.

"Oh darling," she sighed. "I'm so happy." And she was – even if the seven Athenian girls gave her filthy looks and talked about her behind her back. She didn't care; she was the one who was going to marry the prince. He had promised her a topaz ring as soon as they reached Athens. "How handsome he looks," she thought, "gazing out to sea like a young god!"

Theseus scanned the horizon, desperately looking for the island of Naxos. They had passed it on the way to Crete; surely they weren't taking another route back. Above him the black sails flapped in the brisk, southerly breeze.

Theseus was desperate. If he returned to Athens with a princess, his father was almost certain to insist that he really did marry her.

"Should I simply push her overboard and say it was an accident?" wondered Theseus. "What is the use of being a prince," he thought, "if you can't dump a girl as soon as she starts getting boring?"

"I can see land," said Ariadne, pointing across the sea. "Is that Athens already?"

Theseus could hardly control his delight.

"No, darling," he replied. He smiled his most gorgeous smile at Ariadne. "It's a most beautiful little island called Naxos. I know, darling, let's tell the ship's captain to anchor there, and then we'll go and have a picnic, just the two of us! All the others can stay on board."

"Oh, don't be such a bore, darling," complained Theseus.

"But I don't like playing games like Hide and Seek," said Ariadne, with a shudder. "Ever since I was a child I've been frightened that no one would ever come and find me again, and I'd be left in some dreadful place all alone."

"Oh, my poor silly darling," cooed Theseus. "Of course I'll come and find you – double quick!"

"All right then," Ariadne agreed reluctantly. "But just in case you can't find me, I'll be hiding in the woods just beyond the sand-dunes."

"See you later, darling," said Theseus, blowing Ariadne a kiss. "I'm missing you already!" He closed his eyes, as Ariadne scampered over the sand-dunes and towards the trees.

As soon as she was out of sight, Theseus opened his eyes and marched smartly down the beach to where the boat lay at anchor.

"Raise the anchor and make ready to sail – immediately!" he ordered as he clambered aboard.

"What's happened to your lady love?" asked Helena, unable to keep a jealous sneer out of her voice.

"Ah," Theseus turned his most dazzling smile on her. "Apparently Ariadne has an old aunt who lives on the far side of the island. She suddenly decided to visit the old lady. She'll sail on in a day or two, as soon as the next boat calls. What's the matter?" Theseus had noticed a suspicious frown on Spiros' face.

"Do you think I'm not telling the truth?" Theseus asked coldly. "Have you forgotten who's in charge around here?" Theseus closed the fingers of his right hand into a tight fist, and pressed the knuckles with the palm of his left hand so that the bones made a loud, threatening, cracking sound.

"Oh, for the gods' sake, Spiros," hissed Helena. "Don't make a fool of yourself. Anyway, nobody liked her. Good riddance, I say."

Spiros stared down, red-faced, at the wooden deck which was now rocking gently, and said no more.

Theseus settled down, with the girls all round him. "There was something I meant to do ... ." He gazed up at the black sails that flapped above him. " ... but I've quite forgotten what it was." He reached out and tickled Helena under the chin, who squealed with overdone laughter.

"Still," murmured Theseus, with a lazy shrug, "it couldn't have been very important." He lay back in the warm sunshine. "Everything will be all right from now on!" he announced confidently.